LITTLE MISS
BUSY

Roger Hargreaves

D0537702

Original concept by
Roger Hargreaves

EGMONT

Little Miss Busy loved nothing more than to be hard at work, keeping herself busy.

As busy as a bee.

In fact, as busy as a hive of bees.

Every day she would get up at three o'clock in the morning.

Then, Little Miss Busy would read a chapter from her favourite book.

It was called *Work is Good for You*.

And then she would get down to the housework.

She would begin by tidying up,
and then sweeping,
and dusting,
and scrubbing,
and polishing,
until everything was spotless.

She would clean her house from top to bottom,
and then from bottom to top, just to make sure.

She even dusted the bread and polished the butter!

She wasn't happy unless she was busy working.

And she didn't rest all day long, not for a minute,
not even for a second.

From three o'clock in the morning until after midnight.

That was until last Monday.

Little Miss Busy wasn't up at three o'clock.

She wasn't up by six o'clock.

She wasn't even out of bed by nine o'clock.

She was ill.

"Oh calamity!" she cried.

"I won't be able to do any work!"

She telephoned Doctor Makeyouwell.

Five minutes later he was at her bedside.

He asked her to put out her tongue.

He examined her throat.

And he looked at her hands and feet.

"What you need is rest, a lot of rest," he said, with a broad smile.

"A lot of rest," repeated Little Miss Busy to herself.

"Oh calamity!"

There was a loud THUMP!

Which was the sound of Little Miss Busy
falling over backwards,
onto the bed,
luckily for her.

On Tuesday, Mr Strong called to see Little Miss Busy.

He brought her seventy-two eggs.

Go on, count them.

"There is nothing like eggs for giving you strength," said Mr Strong.

By the seventy-second egg, Little Miss Busy was feeling much better.

That was until Mr Strong said, "Now you must rest to get your strength up."

There was a loud THUMP!

Which was the sound of Little Miss Busy falling over backwards, on to the bed, luckily for her.

On Wednesday, Mr Greedy came to visit.

He brought an enormous bowl of food.

"I always find that eating a big meal makes me feel better," said Mr Greedy.

Little Miss Busy ate the lot.

She felt better than ever.

That was until Mr Greedy said, "Now you must rest to let your stomach settle."

There was a loud THUMP!

And you know what that was, don't you?

That's right!

Little Miss Busy had fallen over backwards.

On Thursday, Mr Nonsense popped in to see Little Miss Busy.

He brought her … an umbrella!

"Hello," he said. "I hear you're not feeling well. You don't need a rest …"

Little Miss Busy jumped for joy, right out of bed.

"… you need a holiday!" finished Mr Nonsense.

There was a loud THUMP!

That's right.

"There, you look better already," said Mr Nonsense, and left …

… by the open window.

Little Miss Busy picked herself up.

A small smile formed on her face.

Something Mr Nonsense had said had actually made sense.

She had never thought of going on holiday before.

The more she thought about it, the happier she felt.

She thought of all the fun things she could do.

There was the planning and organising,
there was all the shopping she would have to do,
there was the packing,
and she would have to learn the language,
and read lots of books about the place she was
going to.

What a lot of work!

Little Miss Busy smiled happily.

The following Thursday, she was awake at three o'clock in the morning.

Everything was ready.

Little Miss Busy had had one of the busiest weeks of her life.

Which is saying something!

She had only one thing left to do.

And that was …

… to learn how to twiddle her thumbs!